ROMANTIC SEX TALES

EXPLICIT DIRTY EROTICA SHORT STORIES

SHON GACY, SUSAN STAHLS, JULI MATESON, STERLING KLEMM, CANDRA AUBREY

plicit Press

CHAPTER 1

A SESSION OF PLAY WITHOUT PAY

THE BROTHEL WAS FILLED with an assortment of talents. One of the most popular girls, Martha, was waiting on the sidelines and smoking a cigarette. She wore her blonde hair up in a bun. Her eyes were a steamy blue, the kind that looked nearly gray and weathered with wisdom but was sharp with a hidden passion. The year was 1959. The world was changing, but little had changed in the world of prostitution.

Some of the girls had already found their mates for the night. It was very rare that any of them went on without a customer but there was still a chance that one of them might come up short that night. Martha, on the other hand, had filled up her quota for the evening. She was basically off the clock. The madam of the place would be telling any men looking for her that this was the case. All of the men would be turned away from the popular prostitute for the rest of the night. There was one man, however, who would be granted access.

. . .

The man's name was Henry. He was an out-of-towner but Martha had met him several times. She had to admit that he was her favorite. He had come with a friend named Bill who was known for paying more than one prostitute a night. Henry, however, was just looking at the whole operation shyly, as if he had heard of such places existing but never even thought or dreamed about going to one. The whole night, his eyes had been fixed on Martha. He was merely there to support his drunken friend Bill and give him a ride back home after he was done, but Martha knew that they would connect in a deeper way.

During that session, the excitement of his fun with the women drove Bill a little over the edge. When he had come, he was passed out and remained unconscious for the rest of the evening.

That was when Martha gave Henry the eye, and Henry knew what he had to do.

He had to express himself to the woman who had caught his eye in the place. He stepped closer, his brown hair slicked back and his facial hair low, neatly trimmed. His physique was strong but he looked gentle. , the air about him seemed fragile yet romantic. Martha had never met a man like him during her entire career.

Henry instantly became a friend. Martha and Henry spoke for hours that night, Bill resting on the bed beside them and the other prostitutes moving on to other rooms for more sessions. Henry had asked Martha questions that no man had ever asked her- things about her life, where she had come from, why she did what she did. He asked these things with such sincerity as if he really wanted to know her, and he looked so respectable. What kind of man would ever want a whore that lived in a whorehouse?

Martha couldn't deny that she was instantly falling in love.

"Would it be crazy," Henry said after three hours or so, "if I admitted the fact that I am falling deeply in love with you?"

Martha knew that had to meet again. The two exchanged numbers, offered addresses, gave each other a good time to meet, and they would. It took a long time, such a long time... three years later.

Henry met Martha in 1956. It was now 1959. Within that time, so many letters had been sent. Martha kept all of her letters and she knew Henry kept all of his. The poor guy was always traveling, hardly ever given a break to come back to town and rest for his work. Martha understood the demands of a job. She could wait. Good things, her mother always told her, come to those who wait.

The man of her dreams had called her out of the blue, and now she was waiting for him, in dark lingerie and remaining memories.

"He's here," Martha's madam said from the front lobby.

. . .

Martha came out. She didn't even try to put on airs, walk seductively, or give an eye. Her natural walk was even more appetizing, her lips wet with red and her eyes caring.

Henry stood opposite of Martha. He walked close to her, hugged her, and pressed his hands through her hair, kissing her. His hand was on her back and his tongue was slipping into her mouth.

"How much I have missed you," the man said before picking the blonde up and pressing her against him.

Martha smiled, "And I've missed you too." Running her hands through his slick hair, already getting it messy without a second thought, the vixen smiled. "You owe something to me."

Henry nodded. "I know."

"I feel like we know each other well enough. Please, make love to me."

Henry walked the woman over to her room. He still remembered it well. It was the place he had shyly spoken to Martha, made her reveal secrets about herself that she had never told another john. It was the place where she revealed herself to him. She was ready to do it with him, give him all that she could, and over her wet pussy in a way that she had never offered it to a man before.

Henry was already pulling down the woman's panties and throwing it to the floor.

He hadn't even gotten to the room yet, but with so much lingerie in the hallway, he doubted that anyone would mind.

"Oh yes," Martha said as she felt Henry move a hand between her thighs. They were in the room now. Henry had placed the woman down on her bed.

After locking the door, he joined her and started to remove all of the woman's clothing. His would follow. Martha was helping him, throwing his socks to the floor, pulling down his pants, and getting rid of his shirt over the edge of the bed. She had wanted to see him naked for a long time. He was slick and lean, and she had to admit that he was very sexy.

Henry already knew how sexy Martha was. He had seen her in the nude and he was surprised to see that she had hardly aged at all in all of the time that it had been since he saw her. Her nipples were nice and perky, her ass firm, and her legs strong. The woman looked as flexible as she had been three years ago. They had been apart for such ridiculous reasons and now he would claim his prize.

· · ·

Martha thought she would faint when she saw the man's cock. It was so thick and heavy, throbbing. She opened her legs for him. The man took the cues without complaint. Spreading open her pussy lips, the man slammed his cock into her. No preparations were made before he started to work an effective in and out movement and rhythm. Wow, Martha thought as she felt Henry working his cock into her wet hole.

This man really trusted her. She was amazed. Tears were already streaming from her eyes, both from the hard thrusting and the true sentiment she felt in sharing herself with him.

"Oh god, I love you," Henry said without restraint.

Martha was excited. She rubbed his back, letting him take control. She didn't have anything to prove sexually with him. Henry was well aware that she was a professional when it came to lovemaking, sex, and any sort of erotic activity. This meant that with this man, she could merely be herself, let him take control, and dominate the situation. Dominate, he did, without fail. Her pussy hole was open and yearning for him. As his hands held down her wrists, he pumped into Martha with heavy and fast motions. It was just getting faster and harsher. He pushed into her like a champion yet still gave the passionate fix of a lover. She could feel his energy pouring through her veins and pores. She was intoxicated. She needed him, wanted him, and yearned for him.

.   .   .

Martha's eyes were wide. She was screaming, moaning. Her lips were so wet not only from her smeared makeup but from the overflowing saliva. It was hard not to salivate from the strong needing and wanting of this man. Even as he fucked her hard and drove into her without mercy, she really couldn't get enough. It wasn't long before she flung her legs around his waist and forced herself against him, panting and moaning like an animal. She was going to do all that she could to work his dick deeper inside of her body.

Henry was surprised. Even after the love session, he had seen years ago, nothing could prepare him for how well she would please and satisfy him. Although he had been shy in the past, Henry had had his share of girls, and none of them had pleased him as much as Martha did for nearly 45 minutes.

This was how he wanted it to be, three years ago. He wanted to be united with her, the lovebirds together and sharing each other's essence. This was true love to him, and perfection in the truest sense of the word.

"I love you," Martha said. It was then that she realized she could truly say it after Henry had already said it to her. It was a true expression of love, one that money could never buy.

CHAPTER 2

DINNER FOR TWO
UNSCRUPULOUS DESIRES

"I THOUGHT you'd be the chef for tonight," I teased, realizing that Luke had brought in a chef from the hotel to cook us dinner.

"I may be a lot of things, Ms. Viv, but definitely not a chef," he chuckled. An older man dressed in all white chef uniform gave him a faint smile as he placed the food before us on the table.

This was my very first date with Luke, the handsome young man I'd met on the island of Antigua, while on a business trip.

The food smelled amazing, and just as I'd suspected, he'd prepared one of the local dishes of rice, creole seasoned chicken, green beans, and sweet plantains. My stomach grumbled as I looked forward to devouring every item on my plate. We enjoyed the delicious food, washing it down with some red wine soon after.

. . .

"And now for the main course," Luke said as he rose up from the table a few minutes after we'd eaten. Turning on the stereo in the corner of the room with a remote control, he flipped to track seven, the sweet sound of Mariah Carey in "We Belong Together". It was one of his favorite songs, he'd said. "It's a good song," I agreed with him, taking his hand as he led me to the center of the dining room area, spinning me around a few times, as we danced to the music. This was fun, more fun than I'd had in a while.

"Come I've something to show you," he urged, leading me upstairs. When we got to the two top of the stairs he led me to his room, a magnificently decorated master suite. I almost gasped at the sight of the neatly maintained sleeping area.

As I closed the door behind me, he pressed my body up against its wooden surface, his lips capturing mine with a passionate kiss that seemed to almost sweep me off my feet. "I've been waiting to do this the entire night," he smiled, kissing me again. As we kissed, our desire for each other grew and our kisses became more feverish in nature. His tongue explored the insides of my mouth almost viciously as his hand traveled up and down my slender frame. I moaned out, my body aching to feel more of his sweet touch.

His lips soon left my mouth and trailed downwards along the nape of my neck, sucking hard at the tender flesh around my neck. His hands moved upwards, beneath the thin layer of my dress. My body shuddered with excitement, as his fingers made contact with my warm moist core.

"My gosh, you're dripping wet," he said smiling. His fingers seemed to ripple through me as he began thrusting them repeatedly into my temple of delight. I moaned out, bucking my pussy against his long fingers. Luke finally ended his little torture. Scooping me up in his strong arms, he brought me over to the bed and propped me unto the plush white satin sheets.

He took a step back and his eyes traveled up and down my body, examining it inch by inch. In his eyes, he had a hungry desire filled look. He approached me once again while undressing himself. Firstly loosening the bow tie around his neck, then working his fingers along with the buttons of his shirt, and finally removing his pants last. As he stood naked before me, my eyes seemed to be glued to his long erection, protruding in front of him. He took it into his hands and stroked it a few times, giving me a devious little smile.

I laid in the bed watching curiously as he made his way back to me. "Now for dessert," he teased, mounting me and slowly caressing my full melon-shaped breasts through my dress. My body quivered and ached for him. I wanted him to rip away my clothes and deliver me from my erotic thoughts. And he did just that. Bringing his lips to mine, he plunged his tongue into my mouth, wild and hungry, transferring his immense passion unto me.

· · ·

His tongue left my lips and traveled down to my now naked and fully exposed chest. Taking my beige nipple into his mouth, he sucked it feverishly until it hardened to the occasion, confirming my arousal. I could feel my juices trickling down my pussy and onto the bed, saturating a small area beneath my buttocks.

While he licked and sucked one nipple, he took the other between his forefinger and thumb and pinched it lightly, rolling it between his fingers after a while. I moaned out in ecstasy as he continued to increase my pleasure, sucking harder against the nipple and flicking his tongue over and around my hardened peaks.

"Oh God, now Luke...Now..." I was literally begging him to penetrate my moist core. After he was satisfied with himself, he positioned himself, between my legs. Gently he stroked my moist tender flesh with his massive shaft. His raw meat brushing against my wetness felt amazing and I let out several moans of pleasure.

"You want it, don't you?" He asked in an authoritatively sexy tone of voice.

I nodded my head as my legs shook in anticipation. As he brought himself down upon me, his huge cock penetrated the slit of my pussy going deeper and deeper as he moved. He buried himself at the hilt into my wetness, pulling out almost immediately before thrusting his cock harder into my pussy.

. . .

I let out a sharp breath of air as he began moving rhythmically thrusting his cock over and over into my sweetness. My juices seemed to be oozing out of my pussy and unto his cock, and he enjoyed it thoroughly. Taking my breast into the palm of his hand, he massaged them together as he continued to penetrate my temple of delight. The bed shook viciously banging against the wall as he increased the momentum of his thrusts. The room was filled with the sounds of my moaning and his groaning. Thankfully, there was no one else in the house and he didn't seem to have any neighbors close enough to hear me.

Luke continued to serve me with a series of long hard thrusts followed by some shorter quicker thrusts. Over and over, he plundered my pussy with his cock, bringing about unimaginable sensations between my legs. Finally, with one mighty thrust and a loud thunderous groan he exploded his load of hot semen into my warm pussy. I too let out a long outstretched moan as I summited my amazing climax, my body heaving from the bed as I reached my orgasm.

We remained in position for a while as his cum sipped out of my pussy and unto the bed. Luke leaned in and captured my lips with his kissing me passionately. It was clear that he was fully satisfied with what had just happened. After a while, we dozed off into a deep sleep.

CHAPTER 3

HER LOVING ANGEL

MONA COULD HARDLY BELIEVE that one year had gone by. One whole year since her fiancé Jeff died in a terrible car crash. Ever since the accident, Mona found herself longing for Jeff. She loved Jeff with all her heart, and when news of his accident reached her she almost lost her sanity.

They were planning their wedding for four months prior to his accident. As she lay in her bed, she looked at his photograph one last time before trying to fall asleep again.

As she lay in the dimly lit room, a familiar figure appeared in the distance. Mona could hardly believe her eyes. She straightened herself up from the lying position and peered into the distance, focusing her attention on the figure before her. It almost looked like Jeff. But it couldn't be, she tried to convince herself. Jeff Winters was DEAD.

. . .

She slowly got out of bed and walked over to him. "Jeff, is that you?" This was a moment that she'd prayed and begged for since the day, of the accident. The moment when she would see him again, in her room, in her life. And here it was really happening, yet it was so hard to believe.

"Mona, come here." He spoke to her and she immediately responded. "Jeff?"

"Yes, my love," he responded with a warm smile on his face.

Jeff didn't look a day older; in fact, he looked exactly the same way he did on the morning when she last saw him, before the terrible car crash that took his life away. Wrapping his arms around her petite waist, he pulled her closer to him.

How did he do that? He was a ghost, she thought to herself silently. "Kiss me." He whispered in a husky desire filled voice.

Mona missed him dearly and without thinking twice, she immediately captured his lips with hers. If this would be the last time she would ever see him, she wouldn't make the mistake of wasting any time. She had so many unanswered questions, but she managed to push them to the back of her mind and instead continued exploring the insides of his mouth with her tongue. Jeff kissed her back, feverishly, carrying her thoughts on a journey to an open meadow with the two of them kissing as the beautiful fresh air brushed against their skin.

. . .

Jeff continued kissing Mona while creating a variety of images in her mind. He thought of a wooded glen. Instantly they were standing under arching trees, birds singing and a soft breeze blowing. He was momentarily distracted by the surroundings, amazed this really worked. It seemed Mona was thoroughly enjoying his teases. Her body aching for more as he continued to pleasure her, as only a paranormal being could. He was her fiancé in an immortal form, doing things to her that were unimaginable.

She responded by deepening her kiss, running her hands over his body, rubbing against him. Jeff's body responded, his cock growing hard, his hands exploring her breasts. She moaned softly as his hands rubbed across her nipples. Jeff could feel his own arousal growing as her body responded positively to his touch.

He had not been sure whether this was a good idea, to bring back all of these old emotions, but for months he'd hovered over her silently. Wishing that he could change things, wishing that he could be with her as her husband, instead of being with her as her guardian angel.

The only thing that made him feel better in the whole situation was the fact that he would never let anything bad happen to her. He wanted her to live a long, full, healthy life. Why had he come back tonight? He wasn't sure; maybe to give her some closure, so that she could finally move on with her life. Or maybe he'd come back for another reason, for himself, because he couldn't just let her go, let her move on. Anyway, tonight would be their last night together and he wanted to make it as special as possible.

Jeff continued to serve her with a series of long hard thrusts followed by shorter quicker thrusts.

"Oh, God Jeff...Yes!" she moaned, closing her eyes and bucking her pussy against his shaft. He could feel her juices oozing out of her pussy unto his cock as he continued to penetrate her core.

"I've missed you so much," with that Jeff's lips came crashing down on hers. His tongue swept through her mouth as his hands fondled her gorgeous melon-shaped breasts. The tightness of her pussy let him know that she had been to herself. Tiny spasms shot through her body as he slipped his cock in and out of her temple of delight.

As their lips parted, a soft moan escaped her lips as she beckoned him for more. He looked down at Mona; her eyes were open and she was lustily thrusting her hips up to meet his thrusts.

Jeff quickly increased the momentum of his thrusts ramming his cock into her wetness, pleasuring her beyond belief. He could not control himself; his orgasm was bursting from him before he could react. He threw his head back, crying out in both pain and pleasure at each thrust. His orgasm was incredible, more intense than he'd ever had, and went on for what seemed like minutes, his cock pumping endless amounts of his load into her.

Mona too summited her climax letting out a cry of her own, as her juices flowed out of her moist heat.

As she lay in the bed, next to Jeff, she couldn't help but feel whether she was dreaming or actually awake. In her head, she'd just had sex with a ghost, but in her heart, she felt like she'd just made love to her fiancé.

"Is this real?" she blurted out to Jeff.

"Is the sky real? You can see it but can't feel it, what about the wind, you can feel it but can't see it. Does that mean that these things aren't real?" he responded with a faint smile on his face.

The answer to his question was clear; anything you could see was just as real as anything else. The fact was she'd seen him, made love to him, whether he was dead or alive.

CHAPTER 4

MAN OF MY DREAMS

"LIFE IS JUST TOO SHORT. Take the bull by the horns Raven; you really need to find a good-looking man that is respectable. You do not want to stay with the shmuck you're with now. He does not respect you at all. He is always running around on you and out with his *"Boys"* and he leaves you behind. It's time for you to look outside of the box."

Raven was surprised that Sierra was actually getting sharp with her. But she had always been there for her when Dean was not. She had to admit she was really getting tired of being alone all of the time. Raven wiped her tear-stained face looking up at Sierra.

"You know what? You're right. This time I need to be more specific as to what kind of man I want. I mean if I were to have my dream guy I should be able to make him the way I want him in my mind and then we can go from there and find just the right guy. I am done being second best to someone that just does not care about me."

Getting up from her sofa she grabbed a piece of paper. Sierra looked at her strangely. "What in the hell are you doing, Rave?" She said chuckling. "I am going to specify the kind of man that I want. I am actually going to write it down and then before I go to bed for the night I am going to ask the Gods to bless me with this man of my dreams." Sierra looked at Raven like she had lost her mind

"Really, are you kidding me? You do realize that never happens right?" "Hey, anything can happen when you believe anything can happen"

Raven thought about it and then she wrote down the kind of man that she wanted.

"I want a man that has a nice build, is not too muscular, has manners, and is centered on making my life a little easier. He has to be at least 5'9, green eyes, tan, long black hair, and had a sense of compassion for the days I need someone to be there for me."

With that, they said their goodnights, and Sierra left. Raven knew in her mind that it was just crazy to wish for a guy that would be good to her and treat her like she was the only one that mattered. "What's the harm?" she thought. Folding the paper up and putting the paper in her pajama bottom pocket she did a silent prayer and went to bed. Just as she was about to fall asleep she heard a creaking. Sitting up in bed, she looked around there was nothing out of the ordinary. Taking a deep breath she fell asleep.

Where was she? Raven thought, looking around the room. It did not take long to realize that she was not in her own home. The room was gorgeous - it had cherubs that were part of the molding throughout the room and she could tell that just by the feel of the sheets of the bed that they were Egyptian cotton. As she continued to scan the room she had no clue as to where she was, but where ever this was she had to admit she loved to wake up this way all of the time.

Just as she was about to sit up and continue to explore the room the huge wooden door opened, and in walked a man with amazing green eyes; he had a nice build with a gorgeous tan and long black hair. Damn, there was just something that screamed SEXY to her. She could not help but stare at him, he was amazing. Scanning his body, she realized he was only wearing a leopard-print loincloth, and damn, it did not leave much to the imagination. She could tell that he was so hard but she did not want to lead on that she noticed it.

Pausing for a moment she just realized that was the kind of guy that she asked for when she was writing about what she would like to have found in a man. Smiling at her, the strange man brought in a glass of water and some fruit and toast. Looking down at it she smiled. "I could get used to this for sure," she thought.

. . .

"I am glad to see you are awake you have been sleeping for a while. I thought that after you got your energy back we would do whatever you would like, as I am your servant for the day," he smiled as he brushed her hair away from her face. She loved the feel of his hands on her face they were so soft and warm that she did not want him to stop. "I have to say that I may just keep you to myself permanently," she grinned.

Setting her empty tray down on the nightstand she thought about what was going on. But she really was not as impulsive as she was being right now, but that is alright to be in your dreams right? Raven let her hair down. It was long, and she began to get up as she pulled him closer to her. "Well then sir, if you are my servant for the day let me put it to you this way: I want to make love to you and I want you to show me what is like to have a man truly love someone like me and mean it. My name is Raven by the way."

Smiling she looked into his eyes. She could get lost in them for sure. "My name ma'am is Kelden, and I am here because you made a wish for me." Shocked at his response, she knew that she had to have been dreaming after all things like that never came true in real life. She began to run her hand up and down his shaft. God he was amazing "Well Kelden, I need a man to make love to me and one that knows what they are doing, can you do that?"

. . .

"I can do that and more, just call me your half-naked manservant," he said smiling at her. Laying her on her back he spread her legs going down on her and flicking his tongue against to swollen pussy, he loved the taste of her. It was amazing that someone so beautiful had never had a man treat her as good as he was about to. As he continued, he could feel her hands begin pulling at his hair, pushing his tongue into her pussy more. Looking up at her eyes her blue eyes shimmered and her long brown hair seemed to frame her face she looked like an angel.

"I promise you that this will be the best night that you have ever had." Slowly he placed the head of his throbbing shaft into her womanly core. God, she was so hot and he could tell that she wanted more of him just by the way her body undulated and arched as he began pumping his cock back and forth into her. He could feel her body clenching down on his cock and he had to admit he loved the feel of her. In all of his years of being a servant to women, she was the first one that was pure. She wanted to be loved and did not lust after him for his looks and actions, it was just wanting to feel what it would be like to have a man truly love her. He was going to do all he could to make sure she felt that even if it was just for one night.

As they continued, he counted every time that she came for him. 10 was where they were now and she was still going. Switching positions he rolled over and let her ride him. He had to admit he loved the fact that she could keep up as she rode him he began playing with her ample breasts, pulling at them lightly with his fingers and then suckling them. Just then he heard her sweet moan again as she held his head to her chest, grinding her body on his cock.

. . .

"Fuck. I am about to cum again, baby" He could not hold out anymore, he was about to blow. She was so sexy and he wanted more. But he knew that he had to make her cum one more time and collapse from exhaustion.

"Oh Kelden, yea baby please... Right there"

As Raven arched up he held on to her hips arching his cock into her. It was then he knew he managed to do what he wanted to. She came again, collapsing in his arms. Holding her close to him he wished that he could stay with her forever, but he knew that he would have to make some deal with the gods to make that happen. At least he would have this night to remember forever. With that Kelden left Raven in her bed, wrapped up in her sheets.

The next morning Raven woke up with the strangest feeling; like she had had sex last night. Her hips were delightfully sore and she had to admit last night seemed so real but she knew it was a dream as she looked around, she was still in her room.

"Man what a dream," She smiled.

Looking at the bed she wished that Kelden had been here for real. God, what it would have been like to wake up to him every morning. Just then as she looked at the pillow next to her, there was a gold necklace with a pair of wings on it. Picking up the necklace she began to wonder if it was really a dream or not. Either way, she had a feeling that it was not going to be the last night she was with her half-naked manservant. With that, she smiled, wondering what the future would hold.

CHAPTER 5

THE QUEEN MY LOVER

"YOU ARE VERY QUIET TONIGHT, your majesty. Is everything to your liking?" David's soft voice brought her back to reality. Queen Marisol turned, realizing he was still standing next to her. They were less than an inch apart, and a tiny rational voice in her head told her to step away. But her body took over and she took a step even closer to him. Queen Marisol was the ruler of the island. She never socialized with the commoners, much less a servant boy. But tonight was different when she found out that her husband, the king, had slept with Lady Macmillan. She was furious. She left his quarters, and moved to the other side of the castle, with a few of her servants, including the handsome young David.

Suddenly she found herself wrapped in David's arms, pressed against the white linen of his shirt. She was aware of his scent; a mixture of clean starched laundry, spicy floral cologne, and beneath that, the warm heady scent of the man himself. She inhaled deeply, closing her eyes as the scent triggered a cascade of physical sensations. Never had the scent of a man alone, not even the King, affected her this way. She felt herself sway in David's arms.

She looked up at David, his dark eyes soft in the moonlight, watching her, holding her lightly against his body.

"Are you alright, my queen?" David's voice was low and seductive, holding a promise of something forbidden and exciting.

"Yes, yes. I am." Her voice was a tiny whisper. She placed her hands on his chest; she could feel his heartbeat through the fabric of his shirt.

When David bent to kiss her, cupping her face with his hands, she did not resist.

His lips were soft on hers, gently moving over her mouth. She was used to Paul's crushing kisses, bruising her, his tongue insistently forced into her mouth. David made no move beyond sensually kissing her, his tongue slowly tracing across her lips, soft and feather-light, like the tropical breezes that played around her body.

Queen Marisol was fascinated by David's kisses. He seemed to want nothing from her, no thrust and parry of tongues, no claiming or plundering her mouth, just a slow, leisurely exploration of her lips with his. Queen Marisol felt a slow burn start deep in her stomach, smoldering quietly but steadily.

David's hands cradled her face; she longed for them to be on her body. She ran her own hands down his chest, around to his broad back, pulling him closer to her. In response, David ran his hands lightly down her bare arms, sending a shiver through her body. He rested his hands lightly on her waist, holding her against him. She could feel the pressure of his erection against her stomach.

"My Queen, you are an exquisitely beautiful woman." The compliment, fuelled by the mists of the wine, brought instant tears to her eyes. David looked down at her, momentarily startled.

"Are you alright? Did I hurt you in some way?" David frowned, watching her closely.

"No, you're fine. I was just...it's been a long time since anyone paid me a compliment." She looked down. "I'm just a little drunk and feeling a little bit sorry for myself."

David wiped away a tear with his long finger. "Beautiful women shouldn't cry. Especially beautiful queens." He kissed her cheek, his tongue tracing the path of her tears. "Don't cry. Just enjoy."

David slowly moved his hands from her arms to cup her breasts. Queen Marisol arched her back, pushing her breasts into David's hands, feeling the heat of his palms through the thin cotton of her dress. David returned his mouth to hers, his kiss a little more insistent, his lips and tongue gently probing her mouth. She gladly opened to him, meeting his tongue, allowing him free access to explore her mouth.

Queen Marisol could feel David's erection growing as he slowly fondled her breasts. She ran her hands down, cupping him, feeling the length of his cock with her hands. The erotic excitement of his touch, combined with the heady feeling of the possibility of being caught doing something wrong was fuelling her desire. She squeezed David, feeling him moan against her mouth.

"Gently, your highness, gently. No need to bruise the fruit." He smiled at her in the darkness, his eyes almost glowing in the moonlight. His hands traveled from her breasts, down to her ass, cupping her lightly, gently squeezing and spreading her ass in time to the slow thrusts of his hips. Queen Marisol felt a heat spreading from her stomach, moving down, coalescing in her sex. She'd never felt such a slow burn before; the whole experience was beyond words, as David watched her with hooded eyes. The slow sensual dance he was doing with her was something new to Queen Marisol.

David had slowly started pulling up the skirt of her dress with his fingers, slowly inching up the fabric, exposing her bare legs and finally her ass. She could feel the soft night breeze blowing on her heated skin, feel David's long fingers touching her. He pulled her closer, sliding one hand into the cleft of her ass, spreading her with his hands, his fingers probing her inner depths. Queen Marisol dropped her head to David's chest, exhaling a moan.

David slid one hand between their bodies, reaching for the zipper on his pants. Queen Marisol felt him tugging the zipper down, and felt his hard cock spring free of his clothes. She could feel the heat of his cock on the naked skin of her stomach, poking her as he continued slowly rocking his hips. He gently pulled her panties aside, sliding two fingers along her slit and then pushing them with exquisite slowness into her. Queen Marisol gasped; David's probing fingers finding a sweet spot that suddenly made her stomach muscles contract, almost doubling her over.

"Ah...that's the spot. It's different on every woman, but it's there." David murmured in her ear, as his fingers continued rubbing inside her. She could feel a pressure gathering in her stomach, low down, behind her pubic bone.

David curled his fingers inside her, rubbing her slightly more forcefully; Queen Marisol convulsed against him, crying out, and liquid squirting from between her legs. She was helpless to control herself and was embarrassed at her body's reaction, frightened for a moment she'd urinated on David.

But David seemed pleased, or at least more aroused. His

breathing quickened and his thrusts against her with his cock sped up.

"Oh, Queen Marisol. That's beautiful. Your body is so aware...so sensitive. Did you like that?" She nodded her head against his shirt. In a strange way, she did enjoy the feeling. "Ah, love, and then let's do that again."

David began thrusting his fingers repeatedly into Queen Marisol, curling them inside her, hitting the same spot every time. She convulsed again, each thrust almost doubling her over, each thrust bringing a squirt of liquid. Her body was being wracked with these spasms, each one stronger than the last. She could finally stand it no longer and feebly pushed David's hand away.

"Enough...please. Stop." Her voice was a whisper, her breath ragged and harsh. "That was incredible."

David looked down at her. "You're amazing, my queen." He tipped her chin up, kissing her strongly, deeply this time, his mouth opening hers, his tongue probing her mouth as his fingers had probed her just moments before.

"I want you. I want to feel your exquisite body surrounding mine. I want my cock inside of you." David's voice was like silk, sliding over her, covering her with lust.

"Ahh! "David's voice rang out, just as he exploded his juices inside her and the two of them summated their earth-shattering climax together.

ABOUT THE AUTHOR

Shon Gacy is an emerging erotica author of many erotica kinks and sub-genres. Be sure to check out other books and leave a review if this story got you hot!

Visit my blog at Shon Gacy Blog

Join my newsletter for exclusive Shon Gacy Newsletter

Sign up for Free Stories from Xplicit Press Authors

Xplicit Press Author Updates

Like Xplicit Press on Facebook

Follow Xplicit Press on Twitter

Readers: I want to expand a few of the stories to see where the characters can be explored further. If there are any of the stories that you would like to read more about again, I'd love to hear from you!

Keep In Touch
Shon Gacy
info@shongacy.com